Call of the Wyl

A Destorian Mystery Novelette

By Heather Wohl & Aurora Alba

Call of the Wyl

Content Warning

Contains profanity, discussions of death, bisexuality, & moderate physical violence.

For Rick

Chapter One

Bark Side Tavern,

Wyl Isle

"What happened?" Brutus asked from his rickety bar stool as he readjusted on his tail. "I thought you were gonna get those bar stools with the tail cut-outs?"

Hank, a droopy-eyed wyl, puffed air through his jowls. The raven-black fur of his neck stood on-end as he wiped another glass clean and slammed it on the bar. "Stools cost coin. I ain't got no coin 'cause assholes like *you* never pay their tab."

"*Asssssshole*?" Brutus slurred. He puffed up his chest and flexed his angular ears. The ginger hair on the back of his neck stood on end. "Who're you callin' asshole, dickhead?"

"*You*, ya son-of-a-bitch!" Hank snarled. Brutus lowered his head, baring his teeth, and hunching his shoulders. They fiercely growled at each other. The empty, timeworn tavern was filled with tension and deadly silence.

Hank broke first.

"Damn good, young kit. Damn good. I think you might pass as a half-decent, interrogator."

"Yeah?" Brutus asked, sitting up straight, slurping the last of his beer from his mug. The wyl's tired eyes sagged with the late hour, his exhausted face stippled with the odd white hair. "You'd better hope so if you ever want *me* to pay."

Hank licked the next mug clean and wiped the glass down with a filthy cheesecloth. "A good place to start earnin' a little coin is that new wanted poster I put up tonight. The bounty is 200 gold. You'd pay off your tab and still keep ya' a roof over your head."

"I guess stranger things have *happened,*" Brutus spat, the last word stuck to his tongue like syrup.

"Sure. The world is full of surprises." Hank grumbled. "But I'm guessin' you won't be payin' tonight and I'll be adding it to your tab?"

Brutus stumbled from his bar seat and pointed his gnarled claw back at Hank. "You have guessed right!"

Hank waved away his friend's stupidity and resumed cleaning the evening's dishes that had stacked up behind the bar. Brutus watched as Hank picked up a plate of half-eaten scraps and what remained of gnawed-on noubald steak. Hank was about to hurl the remnants in the trash when Brutus whimpered sharply. Hank glanced up at him in confusion.

"Don't throw that out! Those are good scraps there! The bone barely looks touched,"

Brutus protested, gesturing to the empty bar around them. "There's nobody around. Let me have it. Please?"

Hank scanned Brutus up and down. He noticed how Brutus's cheap, threadbare attire hung from his bones and wondered when was the last time Brutus had a meal that didn't come out of a cask. "Nah, now I gotta put my paw down somewhere, Brutus. You ain't no stray. I'm not havin' you hangin' around here, beggin' for scraps. I'll never be able to get rid of ya."

Brutus's shoulders sank in defeat. He widened his puppy-dog eyes and offered the most pathetic look he could muster.

The chilling, fall breeze howled outside, screeching through slits in the weathered door of the inn. Brutus swallowed hard, not looking forward to another night in the cold, least of all with an empty stomach.

"I could take that trash barrel out for you? You know, since I am headed that way?

Consider it a start to me working off my tab," Brutus added unconvincingly.

The plate of table scraps hovered over the garbage barrel. Hank glanced down at it once more before chucking it in the trash. Brutus let out an involuntary whimper and his ears drooped.

Hank peered up at Brutus's wide eyes and was struck with a pang of remorse. "I suppose it's a start. Take the trash out, and I'll call it even tonight. This is a one-night offer only. Ale ain't free."

Brutus's tail wagged uncontrollably. On unsteady paws, Brutus excitedly romped back to the bar and stopped inches short of the barrel. "Thanks, Hank. You're a good man. You won't regret it."

Hank's tail whipped the wooden wall behind him despite his stern expression. He waved Brutus off and grabbed the next mug. "Don't mention it. I'm *serious*. To anyone." Brutus gave a nod and strained to tug the heavy garbage receptacle toward the door of the tavern. "Don't forget to grab that wanted poster."

"Oh, that's right." Brutus stopped tugging the barrel and turned toward the weathered, wooden tavern wall stippled with nails, each dangling torn shreds and strips of paper. One wanted poster hung intact. Brutus froze, recognizing the poorly-drawn face staring back. He read the text and felt his stomach drop.

Otis Asher of Wyl Isle. No known alias. Red-furred wyl. Four feet tall. White-tipped tail. Wanted for treason & theft. Reward: 200 gold. Dead or alive.

The room suddenly felt as though it were spinning. *Treason*? What has my idiot brother gotten up to *now*?

Hank watched Brutus wobble. "I know we don't usually bring in our own kind, but you could use the coin. He's gonna hang for that."

Brutus nodded and pulled the wanted poster from the nail, reading it again in disbelief.

Hank looked around for a moment and spoke, jerking Brutus from his thoughts. "Gold is gold. Hey, put this stale bread in that can, too, would ya? I don't need it molding all over my bar."

Brutus turned to catch the flying food hurled at him. Once it was in his hands, he could still feel the heat from the cook fire through the bottom of the loaf. Brutus stifled a smile, unable to slow his swishing tail.

"Certainly." Brutus set it on the pile of garbage and hurriedly folded up the wanted poster tucking it into his hole-ridden pocket. He gave Hank an appreciative nod and grabbed the barrel again. As Brutus finished lumbering out the front door, Hank's cheeks rose into a satisfied smile.

Chapter Two

Behind the Bark Side Tavern,
Wyl Isle

Brutus woke up disoriented, his tongue felt like sandpaper in his mouth. The throbbing headache of his hangover pounded in his skull, along with the gut-punch of nausea. The rotting trash beside him assaulted his nostrils and made him gag. His bloodshot eyes drooped as he sat up, realizing he'd slept behind the *Bark Side Tavern* between a few garbage barrels he vaguely remembered rummaging through.

He sat up, sprinkled with garbage. Brutus gnashed on bones, then dusted himself off. Spotting a mold-free bread heel, he snatched it from the ground and stuffed it inside of his pocket, crinkling the wanted poster.

He had to find Otis before anyone else could.

Where the hell do I even start? He thought about it for a moment and decided to ask the wisest person he could think of.

***

"Act right or I'll spank the fur off your behinds!" Mama Asher yelled at her two kits wrestling in the den. As though she had eyes in the back of her head, she scolded them, never turning away from the eggs in a cast-iron skillet. At the sound of her stern voice, the boys broke apart, ears flattened, fluffy, white-tipped tails tucked.

Brutus chuckled as he shut the door behind him. "Mama, don't be scared. It's me."

Mama Asher turned around from the stove and flashed a warm smile to her son. Her aging teeth had lost their luster and her chin was entirely gray now. The burnt orange color of the rest of her fur was a match to his own.

"Bru! How are you? You're so skinny! And what are those *clothes*? I thought you had a job?"

"I do mama, it's… slow right now."

"My son, the lawman. The *thief-taker*. Saving people from the criminals of the world. You think people'd thank you with a hot meal now and then. Those clothes are hanging off of you. Sit down. I'll fix you something."

Brutus's stomach lurched in protest. "No thanks. I already had a big breakfast."

"Oh, so, if it's not for *food*, then what'cha need?"

"Mama, I think Otis got himself in some trouble. He's on a wanted poster."

Mama Asher banged the skillet on the stove and whipped around.

"Merrel, Derrel, why don't you go rough-house outside."

"But Mama, we wanna hear about Otis!" Merrel protested, the black circle of fur around his eye was the singular difference that helped Brutus tell his younger brothers apart.

"Derrel, go show Merrel who can run to the docks fastest? My coin is on you." Brutus smiled.

Merrel's sweet, youthful face stared back at Brutus. His eyes narrowed at his older brother. "You ain't got no coin."

"*Have*." Mama Asher corrected. "He doesn't *have* any coin."

Brutus rolled his eyes, the grammatical correctness of the insult didn't make it sting any less. "Thanks, Ma."

"He's not wrong, now is he?" Mama Asher laughed. "I won't have any of you talking like one of those idiots out there. Merrel, talk right."

"Yes, mama," Merrel whimpered.

"Whoever wins doesn't have to help with clean-up after breakfast. How's that for motivation? Now go!"

Merrel and Derrel bolted out the door and slammed it shut behind them.

Mama Asher sighed, sure one day that door would fall from its hinges. "What's the wanted poster say? Read it to me."

"Otis Asher of Wyl Isle. No known alias. Red-furred wyl. Four feet tall. White-tipped tail. Wanted for treason and theft. Reward: 200 gold. Dead or alive."

"Damn it," Mama Asher snarled. "That boy has always been a wild one. Now he's gone and pissed off the queen? I mean…treason? He always had a habit of getting on the bad side of the wrong people." Mama Asher wiped her fingers on her apron and sat at the table. It had always seated three. Sadly, they never had a need for a fourth. None of Mama Asher's suitors ever stuck around long enough to need one. Brutus sat opposite her and handed her the paper.

Tears formed at the black rims of her eyes. "Put that away before your brothers come back and see it."

Brutus folded up the paper and shoved it back into his pocket. Mama Asher sighed and dabbed her eyes before continuing. "He sent me word a while back, and I heard some things. Gossip, you know. But I heard he was working with those Emerald Bandits. People say they saw him in Desdemona, then in Lagdaloon, pickin' pockets, haulin' a cart of who only *knows* what. I never wanted him working with those boys. Your brother, always fallin' in with the wrong people. He's got those damn sticky fingers and a silver tongue. Now, he's who-knows-where, being hunted like some animal." She chewed on her thumb claw and stared back at him. "You ain't gonna turn him *in*, are ya?"

"Aren't," he corrected, with a grin.

"What?"

"You *aren't* going to turn him in."

Mama Asher swatted him playfully on the shoulder. "I said you young kids shouldn't talk like that. I'm old and set in my ways. Leave me be, boy!"

Brutus threw his arm around his mother, "No, ma. I won't turn him in." He thought about his lie for a moment, wondering if she'd forgive him if he used the proceeds to get the family a little house somewhere far away. A place with cupboards filled to the brim with foodstuffs.

Brutus thought to himself, *Otis is a self-serving asshole with a big mouth. I'd give him up for a roof and a bed. Like a shitty straw bed, with ratty linens.*

They never got along. For as long as he could remember, Brutus wanted to uphold the law and restore order and Otis was hell-bent on breaking it.

Two brothers. Same mother. And yet, no two were ever more different.

"A good place to start is Taernsby. Someone might have already turned him in and they'll have the most recent information on him there at Diresville prison. Work your way backward. Make sure the bounty isn't already filled, that flyer could be old news, then find out where he's hiding out. Maybe the Sheriff there at the prison will have a lead for you."

Brutus nodded. "Alright. One more thing." He dreaded asking her. He hated when she was right. "Can I please have some copper for the ferrymen."

His mother's cheeks rose and she cocked a furry brow. "*Can* you? Or *may* you?"

Chapter Three

Streets of Wannik,

Taernsby

Treading along the path through winding farms, each housing neat rows of plump fall vegetables, Brutus heard garbled sounds in the distance. He walked past rows of corn that stood as tall as he was before coming to long rows of squash and root crops. He plucked a radish the size of a cantaloupe. His nausea had abated and he bit into the bitter vegetable, savoring the slight burn as his canines sunk in with a crisp crunch.

Over the hill ahead, he heard the soft pluck of a lute and the low bass rumble of a drum. He paused for a moment, confused, and then quickened his pace.

It was, after all, his first *Brute Fest*.

He remembered one of his mother's brief suitors telling him about the celebration, warning him to stay out of Taernsby for that one week a year. Brutus was warned of the events and contests each fraught with danger. Despite the warning, it only increased his desire to attend. He doubted his mother would've suggested that he go if she'd have remembered.

Brute Fest was a test of brains, brawn and bravery. It was a place where muscle-bound dwarves could compete against burly barbarians for prizes. Even those not competing were encouraged to participate. Many attendees would leave after the week, spotted with bruises and cuts, all with broad drunken smiles plastered on their faces.

Whoever won the most challenges during the seven days of punishing, painful trials would be crowned *King Brute* for the year. And no one dared to challenge *King Brute*.

Brutus couldn't wait to be among the battling attendees.

The music was loud, but the laughter was louder when he arrived at the edge of where the dirt road blended with the town's cobblestone streets.

An eaflic woman swayed in time with the lute playing beside her. Sweat glistened on her gray skin despite the chill in the air. Her hippo-like features were accentuated with light makeup and her hefty shape was flattered by layers of emerald fabric. The crowd bustled around her. Many others were seated at tables that lined the road, with hay bales along the sides for makeshift seating. Children screamed excitedly as they chased each other through the crowded streets. Brutus stood in awe, dumbstruck by the sight of so many people and so much happening at once.

Was this life outside of Wyl Isle?

He was soon bowled over by a cluster of intoxicated patrons, laughing and punching each other in the arms with fists laden with large rings. They each took turns guessing the kind of precious gemstone that left the imprint on their body. The game was called *Gem-Jam*, Brutus remembered, a competition he'd never had the displeasure of playing. It didn't lend itself well to wyls due to their soft, furry pelts.

He chuckled as they continued past him without so much as an acknowledgment.

Nearby, children arm-wrestled one another, no doubt trying to win their place among the fabled brutes of old. Two burly barbarians sat at the opposite end of the table facing each other. Their opposing skin colors were of no consequence in the Battle of the Brutes.

Brutus watched as the men struggled with one another. The mocha-colored hand quickly pinned the palm of lighter pallor. As the winner laughed loudly, the group erupted in celebration.

The pale barbarian stood as a Bramolt bear sat in his seat. The crowd fell silent. The dark-complected victor stared at his new opponent and exploded into a full-blown belly-laugh. The crowd followed suit and, without argument, the barbarian stood, forfeiting his victory to the inevitable mammalian champion. The Bramolt bear reached across the table, extending his five-digit paw for a handshake. The barbarian clasped the massive paw and shook it before exiting the table.

Several tables had been pushed together and filled to the brim with traditional dishes of the townsfolk. A sniff of heavenly, seasoned meat wafted into Brutus's snout and coaxed the hungry wyl forward like a beckoning finger.

He carefully wedged himself between a eaflic's portly form and the distended belly of an overstuffed frog-like ewanaian. As he pushed his way through the wall of flesh, his mouth filled with saliva. His pupils dilated, swallowing his rust-colored irises.

It was a glorious smorgasbord of food covering a makeshift buffet table, the likes of which Brutus had never seen: esteg steaks piled high, roast chicken garnished with herbs and stuffed with breading, potatoes whipped, mashed, and sliced. There were fresh, pillowy loaves of rye bread. Wheels of fresh noubald cheese. There were muscadine, blueberry and strawberry pies beneath a neat doughy lattice of perfectly-toasted crust as well as cakes with pink, berry-stained icing.

A lone slice of chocolate cake, layered with chocolate icing, sat at the other end of the buffet table. A weak whimper escaped Brutus's drooling mouth. A stunning, arctic-white wyl carried a second chocolate cake up to the table and set it beside the nearly empty platter. His desire for cacao was overtaken by the unrivaled feminine beauty as the shy wyl offered a coy smile. Though they were a few yards away, her crystal-blue eyes gripped his heart in their icy grasp.

The massive, crushing jaws of the eaflic turned toward Brutus, spattering him with half-masticated esteg steak. "Haven't seen *you* here before."

Brutus peered past the elongated hippopotamus jaws, back to the lovely lady in white.

"You ain't from around here I take it." The stranger continued, oblivious to Brutus's stunned expression.

"No," Brutus replied as the gorgeous wyl stepped back into the crowd beyond the table and seemingly disappeared. "I'm from Wyl Isle. I... uh... don't get out much."

"Ah, so this is your first *Brute Fest*?"

Having lost sight of the vision in white, Brutus turned back to the still-chewing eaflic.

His flat teeth pulverized the meat before Brutus's eyes.

"No, never." Brutus managed a tight smile as he tore a roasted chicken leg free from the carcass on the table with his hand, cutting it free with his claws.

The eaflic snatched his furry wrist between his sausage-like fingers. "Then allow me to give you a proper welcome." His face turned back to the crowd-flooded cobblestone street and his baritone voice bellowed. "Fresh meat, good enough to eat!" A jovial smile spread across the stranger's wide jaws as he turned back to the wyl. "You wanna *eat*, right? Then you *gotta* do it."

"Do *what*?" Brutus asked, ears flattening with panic as a sea of faces turned toward him.

The throng of attendees gathered around Brutus, slapping him on the back and squeezing his shoulders as he was yanked away and forced through the crowd. Attendees grabbed their plates and cleared the nearby tabletop. Brutus kicked and flailed in the air as he was scooped up and carried by those around him.

Are they going to eat me alive?, he wondered.

Instead of being laid on his back, as he anticipated, he was propped up on his feet. The lute player plucked a fast-paced melody and the crowd clapped and stomped to the beat. The table shuddered with their thunderous vibrations. The rhythm boomed. Brutus stared at the audience. The bone-white wyl made her way to the front of the crowd and smiled up at him.

"What are they *doing*?" He shouted down to her.

"It's time to *show* them!" Her sweet voice was muffled by the roar of the crowd.

"Show them *what*?" Sweat slicked Brutus's hands. His mouth grew dry.

Shaking her head she climbed onto the hay bale and onto the table beside him. She grasped his furry hands and held them in hers. "Do you know how to dance?"

"Not even a little," he admitted bashfully.

She chuckled and straightened her shoulders. "Watch what I do and do the opposite."

Before his mind could decipher her words, Brutus was being tugged toward her and spun. He laughed at her surprisingly-strong arms. She twisted her hips and her fluffy tail to the beat. Then she stopped, Brutus did his best to repeat her steps, unable to skillfully swish his hips quite the same way. He swayed, rigid and awkward, to the rhythm.

She laughed, "You really *don't* know how to dance."

"I tried to warn you."

She pulled him close and whispered in his ear, "Count with me, one… two… three… four…" she counted on repeat as they stomped on the table in unison. "There you go!

You're getting it! Now have some fun with it."

Brutus lifted his arms to his chest and did a bunny-hop across the table. The crowd erupted in laughter. The beat continued.

Might as well give them a show.

He pulled his dance partner close, picking her up, and spinning her in place before placing her hind legs back on the table. Swept up in the excitement, Brutus dipped her back in a romantic sweep. Her glittering, sapphire eyes squinted in excitement.

"You have a lot of courage, I'll give you that!"

He smiled down at her, entranced by her velvet voice and ultra-smooth coat. He pressed his onyx lips to hers. He felt her body tense in his arms, then relax.

The crowd cheered and Brutus pulled away. He bowed toward the people and then toward his gracious dance partner, who stood with a hand on her mouth in shock.

Then came a new contender, a woman no taller than Brutus. She scrambled onto the table. Brutus smiled up at the muscular barbarian, but a scowl was returned. The woman's long, sweeping brown hair did not hide the furious flush of her face. Brutus panicked. *He realized he had made a mistake.* Where could he run? He stood encircled by a sea of people; he saw no immediate way out.

"Danvy, Danvy wait!" his enchantress screamed over the cheering crowd. Brutus turned back to his dance partner.

The wyl woman he had kissed just moments before, shape-shifted before his eyes. Fur receded behind tanned flesh. Ears turned pink and human-like. Fur morphed into curly tendrils of strawberry-blonde hair.

Panicked, Brutus turned back to the barbarian who quickly closed the gap between them. Seeing her ball her hand into a fist, Brutus raised his arms defensively.

He always knew the death of him would be over a beautiful woman.

As the barbarian's fist connected with Brutus's eye, the world went black and the orchestra of cheers faded into a low hum of concerned "oohs." Before he lost consciousness, he heard a rowdy man in the crowd scream out:

"Now, *this* is *Brute Fest!*"

Chapter Four

Streets of Wannik,

Taernsby

Reality came screaming back to Brutus. His eye throbbed in unison with his heart. Muffled cheers turned crisp as his eyes fluttered open. The world spun, his snout sniffed all of the cooling nearby food, and the sweat of the festival's attendees. He suddenly felt ill. He propped himself up on his elbows and pinched his eyes closed, hoping to relieve the vertigo. Within a few moments, the world came back into focus as the townsfolk and its visitors clanked beer mugs and punched each other in the arms, chest and face with reckless abandon.

"Hey! Are you okay?" A blurred view of swishing strawberry-blonde hair wafted in front of his eyes.

"What *are* you?" He croaked.

"Huh? Sorry, you'll have to speak up."

"What *are* you!?" He yelled, unable to judge how loud he was talking.

"Oh! Me? I'm a druid." She chuckled. "Name's Violet, what's yours?"

"I'm—"

As her face came into full view, Brutus was taken aback. Her pale, pink lips exposed a perfect set of human teeth. Her freckled cheeks scrunched beneath the same crystal-blue eyes that had a hold on him from first glance. He cleared his throat and forced himself to sit up.

"I'm Brutus." He waved her off. "I'm so sorry about getting you in trouble with your... *friend*? *Partner*? Whoever she was."

"What? Oh! *Danvy*?" She gave a hardy laugh. "She's not my girlfriend. It didn't work out between us. Now she's just a gal with a crush."

Brutus, chuckled patting his puffy, watery eye. The swelling was already underway.

Violet placed a comforting hand on his arm. "You've officially been welcomed to *Brute Fest*. None of the men leave without a black eye… or *two*. We find teeth for *weeks* after the festivities."

Brutus widened his eyes in alarm and immediately squinted in pain. *Did she say teeth?*

"Come on. You can buy me a pint."

"What? I just got punched in the *face*, I think that means *you* should buy the pint."

Violet smirked. "Sure, but you also stole a kiss," she added bashfully, averting her gaze. "And no man leaves the festival unscathed."

Brutus nodded, "I apologize for that. I hope I didn't make you uncomfortable. It was not my intention. I got swept up in the moment."

Violet took a seat on the ground beside him. "No harm done. It was a great kiss. Not sure it was worth a shiner, though."

"Oh, it was *easily* worth the *shiner*." He gave her a shy smile.

Violet's cheeks flushed with his admission. The heat radiating from her body, mixed with his nerves, made him want to pant. He choked back the urge, nervous hands clasping each other in his lap. Silence filled the electrified air between them.

Out in the street, some of the men drunkenly sang along to the lute player's ballad. Others walked across a path made of broken shards of glass. Brutus had never seen anything like it. Bloodied and bruised men walked arm-in-arm and women dabbed their wounds before shoving the men back into the nearest brawl.

Brutus watched as a female quichyrd dove headfirst into a brawl, knocking out another contestant. Her beak parted as she laughed. She blotted her feathered skin that peeked out from beneath her obsidian-cotton dress and stepped out from between all of the battling behemoths. She laughed jovially before being shoved, spurring on another attack. She made a loud, shrieking chirp, and Brutus couldn't help but laugh.

How could people be in so much pain and still be having fun?

"So what brings you this far North?" Violet asked, interrupting his thoughts. "Am I right to assume you are from Wyl Isle."

The butterflies in Brutus's gut dissipated, morphing into a pang of guilt. "Yes. *Normally,* I'm a thief-taker but right now my mark is my brother. I gotta find him and get him to safety before the law catches up to him."

Violet's smile drooped and her eyebrows furrowed with concern, "*Wanted*? For what?"

"He, well..."

"What? Did he *kill* someone?"

"No! *What*? No, it was *treason*." Brutus ran his fingers between his ears to calm himself. "I don't know what exactly he *did*, but he's on the posters. If he's caught, I'm afraid he'll be executed for it. He'll be sent to Diresville and tortured at the very least. They are known for trumping up charges and keeping people with minor offenses in there for life. My idiot brother really stepped in it this time… he always *did* have a bad habit of pissing off the wrong kind of people."

He pulled the wanted poster from his pocket and handed it to her. She unfolded it, studied the image, and nodded.

"He sure does look like you. Maybe I'll turn *you* in and get myself a whole mess o' gold." She snickered.

Brutus lifted his tail with his hand showing her the fluffy tip. "Nah, He's got a white-tipped tail. Sorry, but you won't get much for me." He smiled. "I'm the *good* one. *He's* the troublemaker."

"Sounds like your brother and I might get along." She grinned. Something in her eyes gave him pause.

"Why, because you're both thieves?"

Violet stared at him with her mouth open, utterly stunned at the accusation. "What?! I'm not a thief."

Brutus cocked his head to the side, raising his eyebrows in disbelief. "I saw your hand go into that guy's coin-purse when I started dancing. And your pouch is bigger than when I arrived. If I hadn't seen it a million times, I'd believe you. I'll give it to you, you seem very innocent and unsuspecting."

Violet's expression held for a moment before her shoulders sagged and her pillowy lips frowned. "You gonna turn me in? You're a thief-taker after all." Her voice was devoid of the bubbly tone and higher pitch that had been there just moments before.

"I *should*." He snickered a little. "But I'm not here for you, I'm here to find Otis… and to *devour* some of that delicious-looking cake I saw you holding."

Violet's smile returned. She gracefully stood and dusted herself off. "Here. Follow me." She extended her hand out to his and Brutus reluctantly took it, unsure what he was getting himself into.

He watched as her swaying figure shape-shifted mid-stride. Her strawberry-blonde hair transformed into a wiry, white puff. Her freckled skin stretched and wrinkled. Her straight posture curved and hunched over. Her gait slowed to a shuffle. The white tulip-skirted cotton dress was the only thing that stayed true to her natural form.

As the now-frail, old lady made her way back to the makeshift buffet table across the cobblestone path, people parted to allow her to pass. She weakly grabbed the half-full platter of cake, pretending to groan under the weight of it as she turned to leave. A thick orc's hand grasped her shoulder and he spun her around. The mountain of muscle glared down at the tiny woman.

"Where do you—" His eyes grew large. "Oh, sorry, Madam. I thought you were a scamp, trying to steal that bit of cake."

"Oh, *goodness,* no!" She said with a gravelly voice. "It was to feed a lowly, homeless man I met down the road. Thought he might use a spot of something sweet."

Brutus's eyes widened at the raspy voice emerging from the once-young lass he'd been talking to only moments before. He scurried by her side and looped an arm through hers.

"Madam, allow me to escort you. There's all sorts of riff-raff in these woods."

"Oh, aren't you just a *darling!*" Violet cooed. "Thank you, young man."

Brutus gestured toward the woods, "It's my honor."

The orc watched suspiciously as Brutus helped shuffle the elderly version of Violet along. The orc returned his eyes to the drunken brawl behind him, eager to put his flexing muscles to good use.

Chapter Five

Forest of Taernsby,

Taernsby

"Wait, wait, wait!" shouted Brutus, unable to get the words out without laughing. "That *can't* be real."

"It *is*!" She laughed. "Hand to the Gods."

Brutus propped up on his elbows in Violet's modest tent. Furry pelts lined the floor where they laid, with their feet to the campfire outside. Despite the nippy night air, Brutus couldn't help but pant. Violet's cheeks hadn't lost their blush. Violet stayed laid down on her mahogany-colored bear pelt that spanned the entire floor of her tent. The conversation effortlessly flowed over the empty cake platter between them.

"So, what happens if you don't play along?"

"Then they will either fight you or you buy them a beer to replace it."

Brutus feigned anger. "I feel so *excluded*. What will I even *do* without slamming into someone, spilling their beer, and tap-dancing on shattered shards of glass?" His sarcasm was thick. "It just sounds like such *fun*! I'm *really* missing out."

"You won't win a free *pint* if you don't play! Not to mention, you furry lads have an advantage with those thick foot-pads. My feet are all flesh. I'm terrible at it." She added, wiggling her petite feet beside the fire.

"You're a shapeshifter. Why can't you shift into things that don't have fleshy feet? Or shapeshift into something with hooves?"

She giggled, "That would prove how strong and brave that shapeshifted creature would be. Not how strong *I am*. You come as you are. People are there to prove *their* prowess. Not the strength and courage of *something or someone else*. I want the real me to win if I am brave enough to play the game, which obviously I am not."

Comfortable silence spanned between them as he thought about her response.

"You know, I was always told that outside of Wyl Isle everyone hates us. Rumors are that we are *thieves* and women-stealing wizards. I mean, the *last* part is true, but the first part is… *uncalled for*."

They laughed together in the tent, drinking water out of tavern mugs.

"So, what's it like? Being a druid seems like it could get you into a lot of trouble."

"Oh, it does." She giggled. "I used to think it was boring. But, then I moved out on my own. Now, my favorite thing to do is transform into a bird and soar. It's so freeing. It's also a fantastic way to spy on people."

"I'll bet." He giggled. "One could probably make serious coin, too. Blackmail, secret stashes… you could be privy to all *sorts* of things. No one would ever know."

"Wyls have their skill-sets. Druids do as well. Sure, I can shift into anything I have seen and that I know. The downside is after a few shifts, I become exhausted. If I didn't have such engaging company, I'd be asleep by now. I may only be able to shift a handful of times in a day before I pass out, so I usually use it sparingly. But today was Brute Fest, it's all about pushing your limitations and proving your prowess.

"Like any muscle, it gets stronger with practice and time, but even after all the festivities today, shifting was exhausting. Whereas a wyl's special ability is the fact that you could charm the pants off a Bramolt bear. You know… I can shape-shift into a Bramolt bear." She joked, flirtatiously, and winked.

He laughed nervously, "I'll leave all charming to you druids. You play dirty." A smile crept up at the corners of his thin, black lips.

"Oh, and how is *that*?" Her soft waves bounced and she turned to face him. Something about her smirk made his heart flutter in his chest. Light from the campfire danced across her exquisite features. The reflection of the firelight glittered in her lapis eyes. He tucked a stray strand of her hair back behind her ear. As his fingertips grazed her cheek, she closed her eyes and leaned into his hand. He felt a part of himself losing control as an internal battle waged. He fought the insatiable urge to kiss her again.

To keep his lips occupied, he chattered away. "I think I understand you more than you know. You're always able to show people what they want to see. Wanna belong in a crowd of barbarians, you shift into a barbarian. Blending in with elves, you can become one. Yet you had conveniently turned into a wyl, the second most beautiful thing, because that's what you thought I wanted to see."

"And the *most* beautiful thing?" She asked, flashing him a glance that said she already knew the answer.

"Well, she's sitting right across from me." He smiled.

She chuckled and looked away.

Sensing things moving too quickly, Brutus changed the subject. "So, you live out here all year?"

"No, I'm just camped out here for a bit. I'm saving up for a home right now."

"Are you? Planning on buying in Wannik?" He asked, hopeful.

"No. I want to see the world. If I had to settle down anywhere I think I'd love Apex. I hear it's always warm there. So clean and advanced. With plants I can't even *imagine*. I bet it's beautiful. When I was growing up, I always dreamed of living there, amongst the clouds in a classy society."

"Where are you from, originally?"

Violet sat upright "Promise not to tell anyone around here? I don't want people to know."

Brutus propped himself up on his elbows. "Of course. That's not my business, you don't have to tell me if you don't want to."

"No." She sighed. "It's alright. I'm just… a little sensitive about it." She shook her head and pulled her knees to her chest. "I'm from Lagdaloon."

"Oh." Brutus swallowed the lump in his throat. "Did you have family there?"

"Sort of." She turned toward him and wrung her hands together over her abdomen, unable to meet his gaze. She stared up at the starry night beyond the tent. Celestial bodies speckled the raven sky suspended above them. "My mother worked at one of the saloons as one of their... courtesans. My mother had no idea who my father was. I ran away when I was 18. It was time for me to join them or move out, so…" She gestured to her tent. "This is home sweet home, for now. Has been for a few years. On the really cold nights, they let me sleep in the bakery."

Brutus nodded. "At least you have a tent. A nice one, at that. And you have mugs. You probably stole them from that tavern." He laughed.

"I didn't steal them. The bakery is next to the tavern. Sometimes they bring us their imported stuff to try. I just never gave the mugs back." She chuckled. They laid down on the tent's fur flooring, facing one another.

Having locked eyes, they relished the beauty of the moment. Brutus was secretly relieved she hadn't asked him where he lived. "So *that's* why you smell so good. Like sweet rolls."

"Yeah, hazard of working around sugar all day."

"Nothing wrong with being so *sweet*," he teased, nudging her with his shoulder.

"Ugh, that was terrible." Despite the tragic pun, she gave a groggy giggle.

For a long moment, they simply stared at one another, wishing the other would make a move. Brutus studied her delicate features. Heat rose to his cheeks. In the comfortable silence, Violet grabbed his hand. The feeling of the skin of her fingers interlaced with his own made his tail swish with excitement. Seeing his body respond to her so joyfully made her smile. Brutus didn't seem to notice.

"Your tail, is, um…"

"Huh?"

"Your tail is wagging." She laughed.

Brutus raised his eyebrows and considered his own rear before he threw his head back and pinched his eyes closed.

"Yeah, it has a mind of its own."

"It's adorable." She giggled. "Sort of a dead giveaway that you like me though." Her exhausted voice dribbled out like honey to his ears.

His heartbeat double-time as she scooted closer and rested her head on his shoulder. A gentle autumnal breeze tousled her strawberry blonde curls, wafting her scent of sugar and lavender into his nostrils.

The moment was perfect. Yet he was unable to muster the courage, without a crowd of cheering onlookers, to make a move.

Violet fought a yawn, barely able to keep her eyes open.

"Well, it's getting late. I wouldn't mind if you stayed the night. Nothing obscene, I promise. It just gets drafty and cold in the tent this time of year. *Oh*…and I can teach you how to play *Gem-Jam*."

"Maybe… I know *this* is a *wild* idea, but maybe we *don't* punch each other, and just stay like this until we fall asleep?"

"I think I could manage that." She grinned, nestling her face on his chest.

Brutus's tail wagged faster. Both of them laid back in the tent.

Violet briefly squirmed to get comfortable, settling her head on his chest. Soon, she was lulled into a deep slumber at the sound of the rhythmic drumming of his heart.

As the hours slipped mercilessly past, Brutus fought sleep. He wanted to savor every moment he could with her as he memorized her scent and the tint of her skin.

With an aching in his chest he had never felt before, Brutus lay awake. His mind whirled with thoughts and simultaneous excitement and sadness. He suddenly felt a longing for a part of himself he didn't know existed, but was now resting peacefully beside him. Whether it was simple infatuation or true love, he was not sure. What he did know was that every cell in his body relaxed with her softly breathing on his chest. His mind, however, grounded his soaring heart, reminding him that he had no choice but to leave come dawn.

But he needed more of her. More time with her, to know everything about her.

Their timing, however, was horribly inconvenient. Letting her go would prove to be the second hardest thing he had ever done, second only to waking her.

Chapter Six

Diresville Prison,

Taernsby

Brutus walked toward the towering stone walls surrounding the Diresville prison with his ears pinned back to his head. Up ahead, he spotted Destoria's one and only prison. He spotted metal bars across windows three stories high. The depth of the building gave him pause. The side of the prison seemed impossibly long. *Every prisoner of the surrounding continents must be kept inside,* he thought. It was simply too many cells to just be the scum of Destoria. Who else was shipping their prisoners here, he wondered.

His mind darted back to earlier that morning, when he had to do the unthinkable:

leave Violet behind. The trek felt much shorter than it was, gliding on a cloud of infatuation, with his mind preoccupied by his strawberry-blonde beauty. His shoulder still stung from being pinned to the ground for hours, unwilling to disturb her. At the thought of her, he inhaled deeply, still able to smell her scent on his obsidian-cotton shirt. The enchanting fragrance filled his heart with hope. Though they promised to keep in touch, he had every intention of seeing her again as soon as he had rescued his idiot brother.

Past fields of wheat, ones as far as the eye could see, sat Diresville Prison. The new-found surge of optimism faded as he approached the guards standing on either side of the massive wood-and-iron gate blocking the entrance. The air just outside of the gates stunk of mold, sweat and the sour odor of feces. It was a putrid stench, the likes of which he had never had the displeasure of smelling before and prayed he'd never have to smell again. A gust of wind only served to swirl the smell around him like a rancid tornado.

"Afternoon, Porters," he said formally to the two burly barbarians, both in full suits of armor with swords on their hips, stationed on each side of the gate. "I'm a thief-taker. I'm here to talk to the sheriff about a warrant."

"A *wyl* walking *into* a prison? Saves us time, go on in," one of the porters snarked behind his helmet, no doubt obscuring a smug grin.

Brutus brushed off the comment. There were more important matters at stake.

"Thank you." He glanced at each of the men and nodded.

The second guard scoffed. "Saves us the trouble of having to hunt you down later." He turned toward the open-latticed slats in the gate and shouted, "Open the gates!"

Brutus paused for a moment. He knew the world outside of Wyl Isle would not always be kind, but the blatant racism wasn't something he'd prepared himself for. Behind his back was one thing. That was *their* problem. But saying such remarks straight to his face was a new level of disrespect he had rarely encountered before. He stared back at the second guard with an expression of disgust.

"Got somethin' to say, do ya?" the first guard instigated.

Brutus's muscles tensed and he forced a smile. "Nope. Nothing." He was also certain that wouldn't be the last time he would encounter the closed-mindedness of city folk.

The second porter's smile faded at his failed attempt to entice the wyl into acting out.

Brutus watched rumbling gates roll upward, opening enough to walk beneath them. He nodded to the men and entered beneath the drawn gate and listened to it drop back into place behind him, shaking the stone floor beneath his feet, closing him inside like the lid on a tomb. Suddenly Brutus felt trapped. *Caged.* Panicked.

Up on the walls ahead were small, retired torture devices that seemed to serve as macabre decorations hung between a wall of fulfilled wanted posters, each with the word *CAPTURED* written across names he recognized as notorious criminals of Destoria. In the center was a door leading to the back of the prison. With the weight of uncertainty pressing down on him, Brutus's ears twitched with nerves.

He spotted a human in black cotton pajamas behind a wooden desk, staring into nothingness to his left. His hair was disheveled, and his frail appearance made him appear as a ghost of a human standing idly before him.

"Good morning. I am here to see about a warrant. Brutus asked the man behind the desk, fear evident in his cracking voice.

"I'm Don." The man answered flatly. Something about him gave Brutus the creeps. It could be his completely flat-affect, or the fact that he wasn't dressed in armor like the guards at the gate.

"Well, Don I'm looking for someone-"

"I'm Don." The man answered again, to no question in particular. His eyes clearly portrayed someone who's senses had departed long ago. Brutus furrowed his brows in confusion.

"Yes, we have established that. You are Don. I am Brutus." The wyl couldn't keep a straight face as he waved a hand in front of the man's eerie stare. *No one was home.*

"Damn it, Don," a voice barked from behind Brutus as a figure hustled up the staircase from the basement. He hurriedly tied his pants back around his waist and climbed the last step up into the gatehouse to join them. "Can't a man take a piss without you breaking out and causing trouble?" Brutus noted the guard's brawny build and how his armor was barely large enough to contain the mountain of meat beneath.

"I am Don." The human spouted again.

"No shit? Wouldn't have guessed," The guard answered back sarcastically. "Don, get back to your cell."

"I am—"

"Don. Yes. You have made that clear many, many times. Back to your cell."

"Don." Don finished.

The exasperated guard's shoulders sank at his wasted breath. He pointed to the door beneath the torture devices and posters. As Don shuffled back toward it, the guard gave a relieved sigh and nodded to Brutus. "Now what business do you—"

"I AM DON!" Shouted the prisoner as he shut the door quietly behind him, not to be forgotten.

The guard pinched his eyes shut and gritted his teeth. "How can I help you?"

Brutus flashed a nervous smile. "I'm here to see if a bounty has been claimed for Otis Asher."

The guard plopped open a large ledger. Realizing this might take a while, Brutus took a closer glance at one of the torture devices on the wall. The *Pear of Anguish* stared back at him, making Brutus sympathetically shiver.

"Any idea when he would have come in?" the guard asked, not bothering to look back up from the scrawled notes on paper.

"No."

The guard sighed. "Then this might take a bit. Are you family? A friend? A business partner?" Brutus couldn't help but think he was hinting that they had been up to something nefarious.

"I'm a *thief-taker*."

"Oh," the guard shook his head. "One of *those*. I see. Well, take a seat."

Brutus turned to a wooden bench beneath the posters, layered in what he was hoping was mud and not dried blood or feces. "I'll stand. Thanks."

"Suit yourself." The guard responded, flipping to the next page.

Restless and anxious, Brutus ran the pads of his clawed fingers through the fur between his ears and spun around. He inspected the posters, each hand-drawn. Each listed the names of the offender, the age, and their crimes.

From a metal nail, Brutus noticed a wyl that looked like himself. Wondering if it was Otis, he read it to pass the time.

"Dale Kane of Wyl Isle. Known Alias: *Twitch*. Tan-furred wyl. Four-feet-tall. Wanted for treason. Dead or alive." He put the wanted poster back up on the nail it hung from. Not seeing his brother's image he turned toward the wall of the captured inmates.

There it was, the same poster he had taken from the Bark Side Tavern.

Otis Asher of Wyl Isle. No known alias. Red-furred wyl. Four-feet-two-inches-tall. White-tipped tail. Wanted for treason and theft. Reward: Two-hundred gold. Dead or alive.

There it was in big red letters, *"Captured."*

"This is him," Brutus added, as he tore the poster down and handed it to the guard. "Does he seem familiar?"

He scanned the paper and nodded. "Yeah, he's here. Came in yesterday."

"He did?" Brutus was awash with a potent mixture of emotions. He was happy to know his brother was safe, yet horrified to know he was safe *in prison.*

"May I see him?"

The guard offered a scrutinizing glance, sizing Brutus up. "Fine. But make it fast. I have things to do and inmates to apparently strap down with chains. We don't need any more nosey types wandering these halls unattended."

"Yes. I understand. He's my brother."

"I thought *my* family was a cluster of nuts." The guard chuckled. "Follow me." He made his way back around the counter and led Brutus to the stairs he just came from. As they descended the worn stones, Brutus felt claustrophobic. The dimly-lit hall seemed to bear down on him. He knew the tales of prisoners that had made their rounds through Wyl Isle, that those who dwelled in the cellar of the prison were the scourge of the inmates, the most notorious, banished to a life in a dank cell, lost to obscurity.

"When is his execution?"

"Queen wants him alive. He's got a life sentence."

Brutus's shoulders sank. He wished he could make himself even smaller, small enough to disappear and never have to see his brother like this. His fear swelled.

What if they stick me down here? He was sure they could stack charges on him if they wanted to. *After all... who would they believe more?*

As Brutus landed the calloused pads of his feet on the chilled stone floor, the cold sent a shiver up his back. Hackles up, they made their way through rows of cells, soon stopping at one with a curled-up wyl, his face obscured beneath a red fur tail. The guard banged his gauntlet against the iron bar, jostling the prisoner awake.

"Otis, your brother is here."

The mound of fur before them unfurled, exposing a face Brutus did not recognize.

"O-Otis? What is going on here?" He stared at the wyl beyond the bars and then flashed a look back at the guard. "That is *not* my brother."

"What? Are you *sure*?" The guard shifted his weight, looking back and forth between their faces. "I dunno. He looks a *lot* like you."

"I'm telling you, that is *not* Otis!" Brutus snarled. "Where *is* he? Where is Otis?"

"I'm here, brother," the inmate protested.

"See, that's *not* my brother. He doesn't call me brother, he calls me *idiot*!"

The guard stood straight and pointed to the jailed wyl. "That is Otis Asher. Our documents say so, *he* says so. Whatever you're trying to pull here today, stop or I'll throw you in there alongside him."

The strangers hazel eyes stared at Brutus, his sunken shoulders deflating further.

"It doesn't bother you that you'd be letting an innocent man rot in your jail?"

"He's a wyl. The world will be *better* for it. Now speak your peace and get out of my jail!"

The guard walked back up the stairs to the gatehouse.

The wyl behind the bars waved him closer. Brutus hesitated before finally leaning his ear toward the bars.

The inmate whispered, "I'm a friend of your brother's. Name's Theo. He said my family won't want for nothin' if I take the rap. Before this, I was a farrier. I made horseshoes and clip hooves. I've burned every bridge and spit on anyone that ever got close enough to give a shit about me. I got nothin' to my name and a whole brood of little ones on the way. Have you ever been in a small house with eight screaming kits?" The inmate briefly pinched his eyes shut and shook his head, recalling their ear-piercing screams. "It's the only way I can get some *quiet*! *This way* they stop looking for your brother and my family is set for life. I gotta do this for *them*, alright? So don't blow this."

"But you'll *die* in here." Brutus protested, amazed he had to convince someone to voluntarily *leave* jail.

"I have made peace with my choices. Can you say the *same*?"

Brutus felt like he'd been punched in the chest. The question hit a nerve he never knew was exposed.

"So where *is* my idiot brother? Our family is worried. We haven't heard from him in months."

"Otis?" The prisoner snickered. "With *his* mouth? He's always in trouble."

Brutus snickered. "You really *do* know my brother. Any idea where he might be?"

"Your brother is in one of two places: the docks, receiving a biago berry shipment, or the whorehouse in Lagdaloon."

Chapter Seven

The Stikitt Inn

Lagdaloon, Silvercrest

Brutus hopped off the cart and gave the ewanaian driver a nod. The glistening, green skin of his face pulled taut into a kind smile.

"You sure you wanna be *here*? I can take you with me to Enewain. I got family up there that can help you out. You don't belong with the riff-raff of this town."

Brutus gave a polite smile. "I'm quite sure, Cecil, but thank you. You've been a tremendous help already. Give my best to your family."

Cecil tipped his straw hat and lightly whipped the reins of his horse. "Don't be getting yourself killed out here."

As the cart rumbled away, Brutus felt a well of anxiety open in his stomach.

What am I doing here?

As he dusted the hay from his cotton pants, he took in the tiny town. The scent of bile and urine stung his nostrils, just as it had in the prison yard that morning.

An apothecary was stationed across the street from a freshly-renovated tavern. Small shops with produce and other goods were sprinkled along both sides of the dirt road ahead of him. The path itself was marred with potholes and divots.

Otis, you bastard. What the netherworld would you be doing here?

The renovated tavern looked like a judgmental face and windows for eyes and pitched roofs over both sitting like furrowed eyebrows.

Sexy, swaying, scantily-clad bodies gyrated and beckoned Brutus from beyond the second-story windows, hopeful that the fresh client had deep pockets.

The front door swung smoothly as he entered. Inside, lanterns hung from thick beams overhead. The stories he had heard of *The Stikitt Inn* were true. The prostitutes perked up as he entered. *I'm chum in the water,* he thought.

Like hungry sharks, the unoccupied prostitutes wove their way through tables and patrons toward the wyl. A scandalously dressed human gave him a bashful smile.

"Hello there, handsome. Care for some company?" The busty woman cooed, thrusting her cleavage toward him. He admired her dishwater-blonde hair and barely-covered breasts peeking out of the bodice of her pink, flouncy gown. Her hips sashayed when she walked. She was a woman on a mission.

Brutus stood board-straight, unsure what to say. Her enchanting emerald eyes and smooth voice made his belly constrict. Images of Violet flooded his mind and a pang of guilt made his twitching ears flutter faster, like the wings of a butterfly, the stunning shapeshifter's laugh echoed in his ears, drowning out the sultry voice of the woman before him. Her face grew increasingly annoyed at his lack of response.

"Do you *speak* or are you going to just stand there staring at my breasts?" She snapped and cleared her throat, taking a moment to regain her composure. "Name's Darla, by the way. Not that you asked."

"Darla, leave that man alone!" shouted a voice from across the room. "A gentleman like you has discerning taste." The female ewanaian made her way toward him. Stuffed in a green corset cinched so tight her breasts were just inches from her chin, she sauntered up to Brutus. She placed a tacky finger on his shirt and dragged it downward. "A man like you, he wants something different. *Exotic*."

He recoiled from the ewanaian's touch. "I'm here to find someone, not for pleasure. My brother is Otis Asher. Have you seen him? He looks a lot like me. We're from the same litter."

As if doused with cold water, both prostitutes stormed off without another word.

"Would that be a no?" He asked, steeped in confusion.

From the back of the tavern, Harlow, a two-headed crolt, stood stone-still. The broom in his hand was dwarfed by his massive, meaty grip, and a dirty apron hung around his bulging waist. An expression of shock had overtaken both of his faces.

"*Otis?*" Harlow called out over the cluster of patrons.

Suddenly a table of men in emerald-green vests rose from their seats.

"*Otis, you son-of-a-bitch!*"

"*Thieving bastard!*"

The men in matching green vests rose from the table and stumbled angrily toward Brutus. Seeing the throng of angry men, he panicked.

Harlow dropped the broom, lumbering to beat the other men to him, pushing them aside before they re-culminated in his wake. "Harlow take care of Otis. Men no need to get hands dirty." Harlow snarled, snatching Brutus up by the thin, fabric of his cotton shirt.

"*No*, Marlow. Put him *down*. He's *ours*!" Shouted one of the bandits.

"I am not Otis, if anyone cares," Brutus finally offered. The room was silent for a moment before the men spoke again.

"You've fooled us once already, you furry bastard," chimed the ring-leader, stepping forward. His thick stubble and bloodshot eyes warned Brutus that he was dealing with a drunkard, and a slovenly one at that. Strings of what he assumed was vomit littered the man's green vest. "We had to

71

disband because of your nonsense. Exos don't need us no more. She thinks we had somethin' to do with you stealin' all of that damn gold and the biagios. Where *is* it? Where did you put our gold and the damned shipment of berries?!"

Brutus gulped. "Listen, fellas, I'm sure I can bring back whatever it was that my brother took."

"Real convenient. You're his brother who just so happens to look *exactly* like him?" barked one of the men.

"*Yeah*!" The others agreed.

"I'm not Otis. He has a white tip on his tail. I don't. *See*?" Brutus pulled his tail and offered a frightened smile. "No white tip."

The men stood in silence as their drug-and-booze-addled minds fought to reconcile the facts with their assumptions.

"Now, I'm confused. Harlow, take this bastard outside and do what you do best. Tear this son-of-a-bitch limb-from-limb!"

Harlow nodded his heads and turned around, exiting with Brutus in tow, passing through the front door as the men inside screamed.

"We would be disbanded if it wasn't for you!"

"You're gonna pay!"

"Rip his nuts off first!"

"Sit on him, Harlow!"

Powerless in Harlow's grip, Brutus listened on at the myriad of drunken fools shouting for his life to come to a tragic end. The thief-taker furiously wiggled and writhed, trying to squirm out of the crolt's oafish grasp, to no avail. Moments later, Harlow set him down on top of a fresh mound of tilled earth and a crudely carved stone beside it.

Brutus was set on the dirt mound and panted frantically.

"How many times do I have to say it, I'm not Otis, please don't—"

"Harlow know you is not Otis. *That* Otis," he said, pointing to the ground.

Confused, Brutus took a step back toward Harlow and faced the crudely-carved stone. The crolt dropped to his knees with a loud thud, tears welling in his eyes. Seeing the odd display, Brutus's head turned to look at the fresh mountain of earth beneath him. On the stone beside him, scrawled in a sort of crude finger painting, he could barely make out the words, "Otis" and "Sorry"

Brutus's heart skipped a beat.

No, it can't be.

"P-please tell me this isn't Otis," He begged, his voice cracking with emotion.

Tears streaked down the cheeks of both of Harlow's morose faces.

"My brother is…" Brutus couldn't bring himself to say the word. "No!" Brutus shouted. "He's not dead! Tell me he's not dead!"

Brutus flew into an uncontrollable rage. Harlow choked back a sob.

"Did… did you do this?" Brutus barked, balling his hands into fists.

Harlow solemnly nodded his heads.

Throwing all sense and safety aside, Brutus lunged at Harlow, chomping his teeth into the tender flesh of the crolt's muscular forearm. Harlow yelped, whipping his arm away before grabbing Brutus by the scruff of his neck. Brutus's limbs suddenly went limp, not cooperating with the instructions of his brain. His tail tucked between his legs. An overwhelming sense of loss and dread washed over him.

Not his brother. Not Otis.

After looking at the bloody bite-mark on his arm, Harlow somberly stared at the wyl. "Harlow is sorry. It… *accident*. Harlow just want to scare him."

Brutus's eyes welled with tears. He always knew one day he'd bury his brother, but it seemed that the deed had already been done *for* him.

Sobs flooded to the surface, boiling over into inconsolable grief. His lip quivered as a stream of tears he was afraid would never stop trickled down his furry face. Harlow released him back to the soil Otis had been shallowly buried beneath. With trembling hands, Brutus touched the stone, tracing his fingers along the letters of Otis's name.

"Why, Harlow?! What… happened?!" He finally asked, entranced by the crudely etched grave marker.

"Otis was *mean* to Harlow. Harlow just want to *scare* Otis and tell him to stop, but he ran away. His cart crash. He flew. He land. *Crack.* Harlow tell him to be nice or else. Otis cry he want apotha… apotha…"

"*Apothecary?*" Brutus asked, helping out the struggling crolt.

"Yes. Then Otis stop breathing. Harlow thought Otis passed out, but when Harlow listen, only hear crack in his chest. No thump-thump." Harlow's sobs made his words almost incomprehensible. "I no mean to kill Otis. Otis *mean,* but Otis was still *friend.* Harlow want him to stop making jokes that Harlow ugly!"

Painful silence.

While Otis tried to absorb the information, the guilt-ridden crolt sobbed, one head in each of its massive hands.

Brutus understood what he was saying: *It was an accident.*

"So, let me make sure I have this straight: you were chasing my brother. He crashed his cart and hurt himself. You tried to scare him and wouldn't let him go to the apothecary… and he died. Then you buried him here and put his name on the stone?"

Harlow nodded. "Harlow took cart and put it deep in the woods so no one know, but keep his things, just in case." The crolt waved him to the back of the tavern where the garbage was heaped into bins. Behind the barrels sat a half-empty sack. Harlow plopped it in front of Brutus.

"Harlow no want it to go to the ladies. Harlow share it with the inn keeper. He kind to Harlow. But Brutus deserve the rest. Forgive Harlow. Harlow mean no harm."

Brutus stared at the open bag bulging with gold coins. Despite the heartbreaking circumstance, his jaw dropped.

"Someone will be certainly looking for this amount of gold. I can't take this."

Harlow picked up the bag and forcefully handed it to Brutus. "Harlow need you take it. Harlow have nightmares about breaking Otis. Harlow need them to stop. Please make them stop."

Brutus suddenly felt betrayed by his own emotions. He pitied the crolt. "Fine, Harlow. I'll take it." He wiped his eyes and stood more erect. "I am taking this with me. It'll go to our family."

Harlow returned to the grave marker and sat beside it. "Otis so funny, except when he mean."

Brutus grabbed the bag and dragged it along the ground toward the grave, taking a seat on the opposite side of the gravestone. "He bullied me, too. I was the runt of the litter. He was definitely the leader of the pack." He chuckled despite the tears in his eyes. "I always knew that *mouth* of his was going to get him in trouble one day. I hate that I was right."

Harlow reached his arm out, bitten and bleeding, toward Brutus and patted the vulnerable wyl on the knee.

"He deserves a proper burial, Harlow. I'm gonna need that cart you stashed away in the woods, a spare wheel, and a good horse to bring him home."

The crolt nodded. "Harlow help you bring him back home, where Otis belong."

Chapter Eight

Community Graveyard,

Wyl Isle

Rain thrummed against Brutus's fur as he sat beside the wooden box holding his brother's remains. His mother, completely beside herself, had come and gone from the funeral service, clutching the furry hands of Merrel and Derrel. The funeral had finished, but the war inside Brutus still raged. Instead, white-hot anger was all he could feel.

He paced, wearing a muddied trail along the edge of the grave-site. His black, silk-lined suit was drenched. His upright collar did little to protect him from the weather. His jaw was tight, fists were balled, knuckles white. His claws dug into the pads of his hands.

"You stupid asshole," Brutus shouted at the casket. "I told you falling in with those bastards would get you killed. That, and your smart mouth. You just couldn't shut it, could you? Marlow told me everything. I believe him. He never would've hurt you on purpose. You didn't have to run!"

Tears mixed with the rain on his cheeks. He thought to the letter in his pocket, no doubt drenched by now. He rose and walked to a painted horse whose skin twitched with the patter of heavy raindrops. It waited patiently, tethered to a tree near some ancient-looking headstones. From its saddlebag, he tugged a massive, muddy burlap bag. Dragging it along the ground, he went back to the burial site. He hesitated for a moment, then hurled it in, atop Otis's casket.

"I found your stupid drawing with the biagio berries you hid. Didn't take much of a detective to figure it out. Ma would've been ashamed to know you were involved in the dikeeka trade, swindling the swindlers. And for what? You had us! It's not like you had nothing to lose! You had us!"

Brutus's voice cracked, face contorting with the pain. "I hate you for what you did. I'll never let Ma know. Or Merrel or Derrel. They don't deserve any more heartache after you up and disappeared on them. You'll stay the martyred son. But I'll know. I'll always know you were just a greedy bastard." He wiped his eyes. Thunder cracked in the distance. He tugged the note from his back pocket and unfolded it in the rain. He glanced at the signature:

Your Violet.

"You'd have liked her, Otis. She's way too beautiful for me, but for some reason she likes me. She really likes me."

He turned from the grave, folding the parchment back up and tucking it back in his pocket. "The worst part of all of this is… I miss you, brother." He stifled a sob and walked back to his horse. He spoke over his shoulder, his voice wavering with emotion. "Watch over us, okay? I know who you really were. You're not in the Nether. You are in the Ethereal Sanctum. And if you get any favors up there, throw them our way. It's the least you could do after all you put us through."

He untied the tether and tucked the rope in a saddlebag. With an awkward leap, he hoisted himself up to the saddle with the stirrup. As he nestled in, he looked back over the rectangular crevasse in the dirt and waved for the waiting staff across the field to fill it in. As he rode away, drops of rain wound their way through the carved letters of his headstone.

It read:

Otis Asher.

Truly one of a kind.

Epilogue

Wannik,

Taernsby

A month passed since their night beneath the stars. Violet had been on his mind every day. Brutus was now a well-manicured, polished gentleman, dressed in fine clothes. In black obsidian-cotton shirt and pants, topped with a silken purple vest, Brutus strutted down the road toward Wannik. The sleepy town seemed different; no long tables or straw benches in the streets, no brawling behemoths or live music. The quaint town was deathly quiet.

As he walked toward the tiny bakery along the main thoroughfare that ran through town, his heart pounded in his chest, his wagging tail unceasing.

Stopping in the doorway, he saw her. His love. Kneading dough with a dusting of flour on her rose-tinted cheek. He felt his aching heart thunder back to life.

He smiled to himself, unsure how he'd make his reintroduction. In his mind, he'd whisk her into his arms as soon as he saw her. But, in reality, he hesitated. So many times he had imagined the reaction to seeing her again. He simply stood, silent in the doorway, stumbling over what to say. His mind skipped from thought to thought like a speedy game of Gem-Jam.

Would she remember him? Would she be as happy to see him as he was to see her? What if she wasn't?

Thoughts whirled in his mind. All came to an abrupt halt as her blue eyes landed on him. Joy danced on her face. It was an echo of his own expression. Warmth grew in his chest and he was certain this was the real thing. His future stood before his eyes, her joyous expression glowing with excitement. He wanted the moment to last, the moment when his forever stared back at him with pure, unadulterated joy. Life as they knew it would never be the same. In fact, they both knew from that day forward, it would be better together.

About the Author

Heather Wohl, co-owner of Rusty Ogre Publishing, also coordinates a laboratory based out of Wyoming. She is the author of The Illuminator Saga and Escape from Sugarland also has other pen names (Aurora Alba for romance, and H.M. Wohl for horror).

An avid storyteller since childhood, Heather has always enjoyed spinning fantastical tales. She is a proud supporter of chronic illness support, mental health awareness, and Pit Bull advocacy. Heart and soul are poured into every page of her work, and she looks forward to entertaining you.

Creature Glossary

Aestuo Quichyrd: *(Ah-ee-stoo Kwih-chard)* A hybrid of bird and human with armored feathers, these bird-humans are battle-ready. They have talon-like hands and a beak.

Akiah: *(Ahh-kai-uh)* Often mistaken for demons, a once-forbidden species, the akiah people have been responsible for carrying out various atrocities under the rule of Master Tempest. With human body shape and features, their defining trait is their ram horns and crimson eyes.

Azure shifters: *(Ah-zur Shif-turs)* These underwater creatures have the face and upper torso of a human, and a fish-like tail for legs. Its golden horns glitter below the surface, luring its prey to the water's edge so they can attack. White eyes and scaly skin are another hallmark of the shifter. Unable to speak or be reasoned with, this remains one of the most deadly creatures in Destoria.

Barbarian: Larger than humans, barbarians are known for their large stature and muscular build. Ideal fighters and human-like features make these characters a staple.

Black-Eyed Beings: Creations of Ceosteol who are imbued with her magical essence, having entered unwillingly into a soul-bond with her. These creatures are an extension of her, controlled by her dark magic.

Bramolt Bear: *(Brahm-olt Bear)* Like a polar bear, these massive fur-covered bears fight with their 3-inch long talons and walk upright. Unable to speak the human language, these bears are both lovable and formidable.

Crolt: (Kruhlt) Two-headed giant. Barely able to fit through doorways, these creatures have two functioning heads that work independently of one another. Their shared body is massive and muscular, making these giants a solid protective force. However, their intelligence is one step above that of a symph.

Dwarf: Dwarves are typically three feet tall with red hair. Both men and women of this species grow beards. They are typically ornery in nature.

Eaflic: *(Ee-flick)* Hippo-human hybrid. With gray skin and a massive snout, these creatures are docile until threatened. With rounded ears and a flicking tail, these creatures are undeniably lovable.

Elf: Elves have the features of a human, but typically have a yellow tint to their skin and pointed ears. Adept at magic, elves are typically upper class.

Esteg: *(Ess-teg)* Sentient deer. Estegs are voracious readers and intelligent. They can speak and comprehend spoken and written words. Their unusual horns (which both the male and female of the species grow) are neon green with healing powers. They are often poached for their antlers.

Ewanaian: *(You-way-nee-an)* Frog people. These creatures are a blend of humans and frogs. With slick, green skin and a tacky tongue, these creatures walk and talk like human beings. When startled, their response is to faint and pass gas as a biologically-programmed deterrent.

Frumlan: *(From-lin)* Sentient wolf/bird hybrids. Larger versions of symphs. With a wolf-like face and furry feathers along its body and wings, these creatures can walk, talk and fly with ease.

Goblin: Goblins are people short in stature (averaging about 2.5 feet in height) with large noses. Sly, cunning and often reclusive. Their fondness for gold keeps them from hiding away completely.

Grindylow: *(Grin-dee-low)* They have a long face with rows of muskie-like teeth and eyes similar to an alligator. They have thin human bodies, often pale, with webbed extremities that create swift, fluid movements. They have winding ibex-type head horns and long claws to shred prey. Used to pull ships along on windless days, Grindylows are working creatures that are best never seen.

Half-Elf: Human and elf hybrid with often-blunted ear tips. With lightly yellow-tinged skin, it is truly a flip on a coin as to if they inherit magical abilities from their elvish side.

Human: *(Hue-mon)* With varied skin tones and averaging five feet eight inches in height, humans' greatest gift is their passion and ability to love.

Inelm: *(In-elm)* These woodland creatures live inside of host tree trunks and pry themselves away when danger or disrespect occurs. They are a proud and communicate through a network of roots below ground.

Kleax: *(Clee-ax)* Lion and human hybrids. This creature is known for their long manes, flitting tail and uneven temperament. Fur covers them and long claws make them formidable fighters.

Orc: With skin in various shades of green, orcs are muscle-bound brutes with a reputation for being strong, fearless warriors. They have thick bottom-row incisors that jut out past the lip.

Pleom: *(Plee-ohm)* Miniature dragonlings. Pleoms are small dragons that live for an average of 8 years. Their scaly skin comes in various colors and their tiny claws are adept at lock-picking, making them an ideal companion for thieves. Pleoms typically prefer to spend their time with estegs who can heal them after their clumsy exploits.

Quichyrd: *(Kw-itch-urd)* A generic bird-human hybrid. Unarmored feathers and no proclivity toward magic. These creatures have a varied appearance, but always with a beak and taloned hands.

Raakaby: *(Ray-kah-bee)* Rabbit-bird hybrids bred for meat. These adorable, poisonous creatures produce a hallucinogenic saliva that is used in dikeeka. More than one bite is fatal.

Semdrog: *(Sehm-drog)* Lizard-human hybrid. These lizard people have skin flaps on their heads and scales. Their eyes have slit pupils, but otherwise they have human features.

Symph: *(Simf)* A small wolf/bird hybrid. They are colorful creatures with a wolf-like face and snout equipped with wings and paws. They are small enough to land in your hand and howl instead of chirp.

Tailed Infernals: An abomination created by Ceosteol, these zombified creatures are two wolves crudely stitched together with a snake tail. Dangerous and decaying, they can be taught and controlled through Ceosteol's soul bond (which she shares with all of her undead atrocities).

Tenebris Quichyrd: *(Ten-ee-bris Kwitch-urd)* Magical Bird-human hybrid. Tenebris Quichyrds are a species of bird people who are gifted in magic. Rare as they are, they are known for causing havoc within the isle, often despised. While not equipped with armored feathers, they wield magic, making them dangerous.

Tundra Goblins: *(Tun-druh Gob-lihns)* These snow-white creatures are violent, seeking warmth in the merciless cold of Evolt. They kill and burrow in their prey. Their fur is highly sought-after and valuable. With long fangs that stick out past their lower lip, these creatures are the perfect combo of cute-and-deadly.

Undead: Reanimated corpses. Undead species of any creature, humans being extra susceptible. Most often the undead is a creation from black magic wielders, which is a strictly forbidden magic, only used by nefarious mages.

Landigo: *(Lahn-dig-oh)* Leopard-human hybrid. Equipped with a graceful tale and fur-covered forms, these spotted beings are known for their quick temper. With a leopard face, these creatures seem to be a welcome addition to the colorful creature variations of Destoria.

Wyl: *(Wy-uhl)* Often known for thievery, and superior lovemaking skills, wyl's are a staple of Destoria. While most wyl's spend their time on *Wyl Isle*, others lie, cheat and steal their way across the rest of Destoria. They come in a variety of colors. Their hallmark face and pointed ears make them easy to spot.

Reviews

If you could take the time to leave an honest review after you've read this book, we at Rusty Ogre Publishing would *greatly* appreciate it. We respect your time and promise it doesn't *have* to be long and eloquent. Even a few words will do!

As a small publishing house, every review helps others determine if this book is right for them and greatly increases our chances of being discovered by someone else who might enjoy it.

More From Rusty Ogre

The Billionaire's Assistant

Book one of the New England Billionaire's Series. Available worldwide in ebook, paperback, hardcover. Audiobook releasing in May of 2024.

Welcome to New England, home of scenic beaches, dazzling autumn foliage, and swoon-worthy affluent billionaires. Hindered by a broken arm, Eric Salko's life is upended when the VP of his investment firm, Rob, hires him a temporary new personal assistant. The moment the stunning employee enters his palatial Greenwich, Connecticut estate, all bets are off.

With her life in shambles, Kira Blumquist is desperate to make the most of her lucky break, but the growing attraction to her new boss threatens to jeopardize everything. Like a moth to a flame, she soon secretly finds herself yearning for his forbidden touch.

Odessa Alba's sensual series debut sizzles with smoldering heat, opulence, and a heartwarming HEA.

The Ugly Sweater
PARTY
A FORCED PROXIMITY ROMANCE NOVELLA
AURORA ALBA &
ODESSA ALBA

The Ugly Sweater Party

By Aurora Alba & Odessa Alba
Available in paperback, ebook, & audiobook.

Ascending to a holiday party on the thirty-second floor of a Manhattan skyscraper, the building's only elevator breaks down, trapping grinchy curmudgeon "Nasty Nate" DuPont and the stubborn Director of Finance, Twila Henderson, inside. With maintenance workers en route, Twila and Nate struggle to stay civil. As hideously dressed co-workers mingle feet beyond their blocked exit, stuffed emotions bubble to the surface over the captive duo's seemingly forgotten past.

Bursting with heat and humor, this is a third-person a spicy standalone contemporary romance novella for fans of forced proximity, enemies-to-lovers, workplace romance, grumpy boss, holiday romance, & romantic comedy tropes.

From Ashes
BOOK ONE OF THE ILLUMINATOR SAGA
Heather Wohl

From Ashes

**Book One of the Illuminator Saga
By Heather Wohl**
Available worldwide in all formats.

She's broken. She's dangerous. She wants revenge. And she has nothing left to lose. Elf blacksmith, Quistix, suffers a tragic loss the night a bandit invades her humble Bellaneau home in search of "The Illuminator." After months of crushing loneliness, the disheveled half-elf is out for blood, seeking revenge on the man who shattered her once-contented life and answers about why this alleged Illuminator is so highly sought-after. A wounded wyl, a brilliant esteg, and child-like dragonling soon join her on her cross-country adventure, banding together in a riotous, misfit crew.

But Destoria is a dangerous place. The isle is bursting with clever hybrid creatures, floating cities, treacherous backstabbers, drug-addled bandits, and the Isle's sadistic, new queen: Exos Tempest.

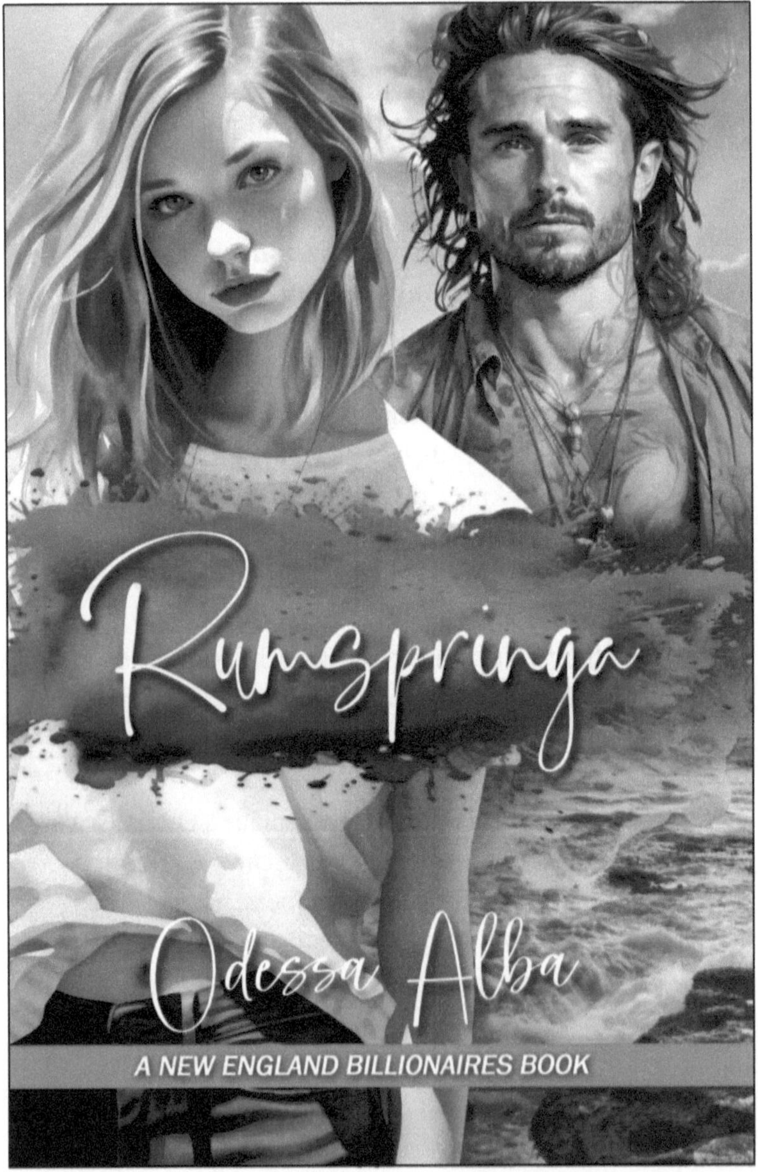

Coming Soon!
Rumspringa
Odessa Alba
A NEW ENGLAND BILLIONAIRES BOOK

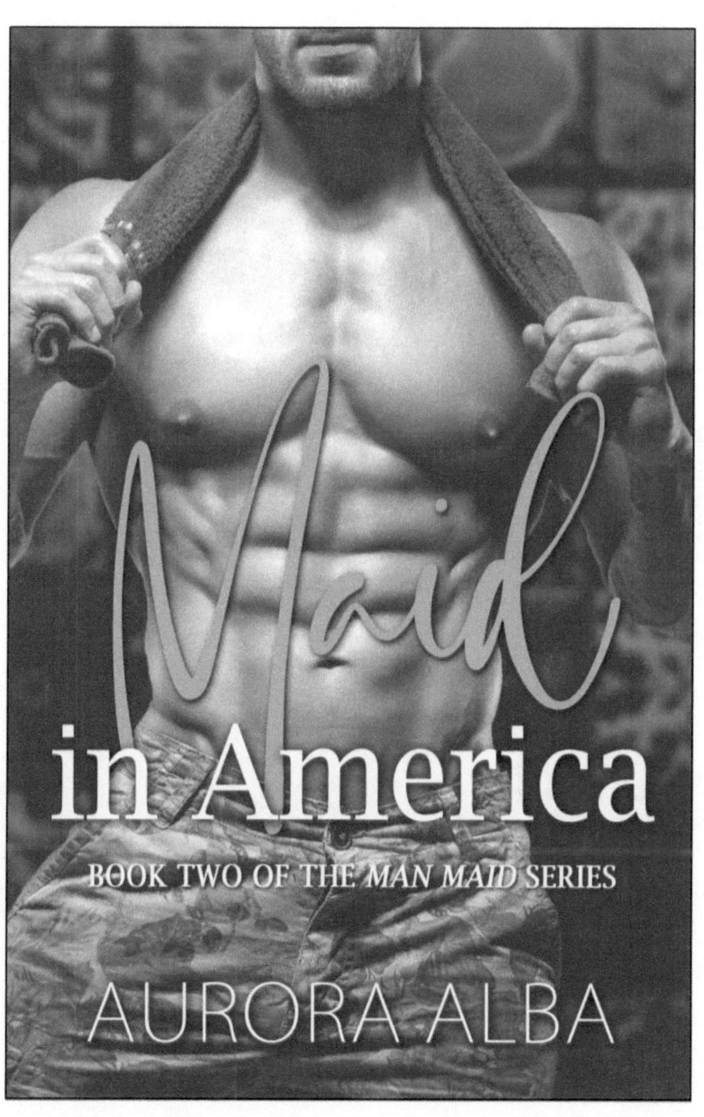

Maid
in America
BOOK TWO OF THE MAN MAID SERIES
AURORA ALBA

THE
Undead Queen
BOOK THREE OF THE ILLUMINATOR SAGA
Heather Wohl